The Magic School Bus®

STICKER STORYBOOK
Dinosaur Rescue

Arnold   Ralphie   Keesha   Phoebe   Carlos   Tim   Wanda   Dorothy Ann   Ms. Frizzle   Liz

Written by Jenne Simon
Illustrated by Carolyn Bracken

Based on *The Magic School Bus* books
written by Joanna Cole and illustrated by Bruce Degen

Sincere appreciation to Dr. Carl Mehling

ISBN 978-0-545-49754-1

12 11 10 9 8 7 6 5 4 3 2 1   13 14 15 16 17 18/0

Printed in Malaysia   106
First printing, April 2013

SCHOLASTIC INC.

Ms. Frizzle's class is always fun.
And every day brings new surprises.

Today we are learning about dinosaurs.
And Ms. Frizzle has a big surprise for us.

Use your stickers to decorate Ms. Frizzle's classroom.

We hop on the bus and it starts to change.
We are going back in time.
"Dinosaurs lived millions of years ago," D.A. says.

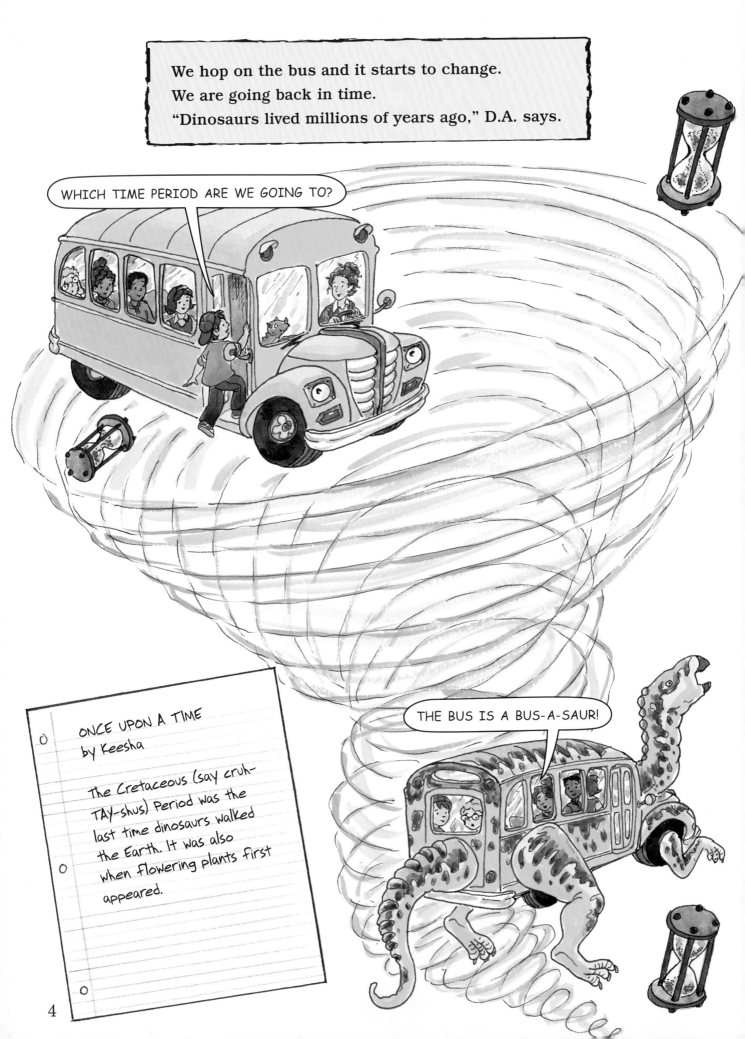

We woosh out of the bus.
We are inside dinosaur eggs.
We land in a nest.

SASSAFRAS

WILLOW

PACHYCEPHALOSAURUS

REDWOOD

PARASAUROLOPHUS

DINOTIME

HORSETAILS

MAGNOLIA

Use your stickers to decorate the landscape.

Soon all the eggs start to hatch.
Baby dinosaurs come out of their eggs, and we hatch out of ours!
Suddenly, Ms. Frizzle waves good-bye.
Uh-Oh! We're on our own.

THIS EGGSHELL IS REALLY THICK.

IT'S A GOOD THING WE CAME PREPARED!

DINO DAYCARE
by Phoebe

Some mother dinosaurs used sand and soil to build their nests. They piled leaves on top of their eggs to keep them warm.

Phoebe makes friends with a baby dinosaur.
"His mouth looks like a duck's bill," she says.
"Let's call him Quacker!"
"That quacks me up!" says Carlos.

WHAT'S THAT IN THE SKY?

THEY LOOK LIKE FLYING REPTILES.

THEY LOOK LIKE TROUBLE!

Use your stickers to decorate the landscape.

Some pterosaurs give us a scare.
The adult dinosaurs try to protect their babies.

pages 2-3

pages 6-7

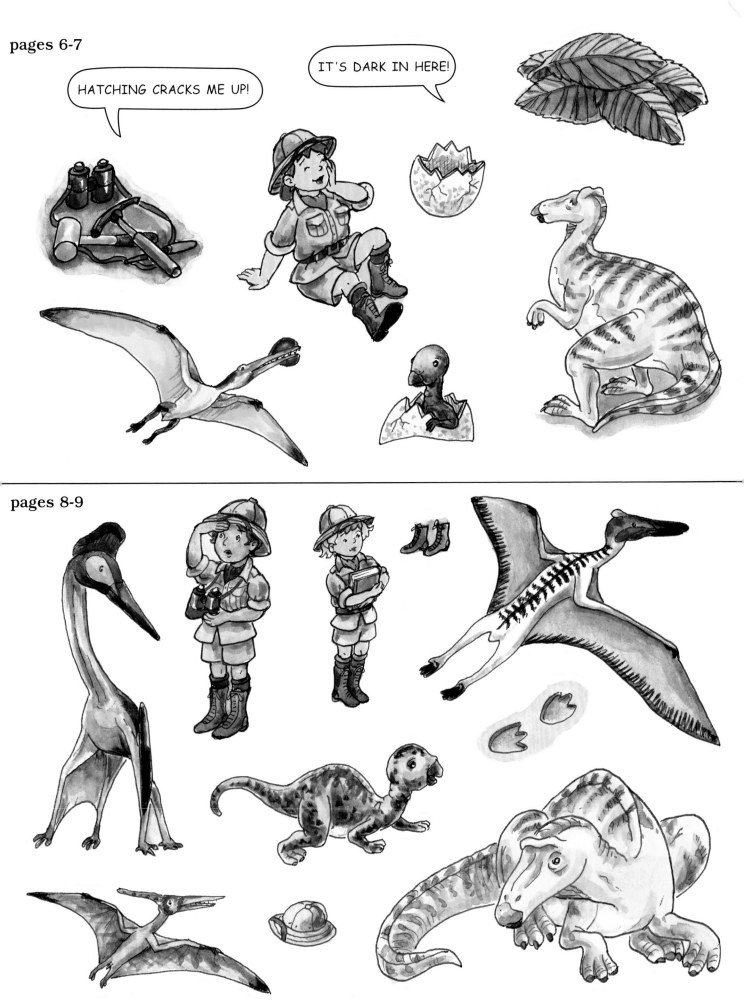

pages 8-9

DINO TIMELINE

245 MILLION YEARS AGO	TRIASSIC PERIOD — DINOS EVOLVE
208 m.y.a.	JURASSIC PERIOD — Birds evolve
145 m.y.a.	CRETACEOUS PERIOD — DINOS die out
65 M.Y.A. TO NOW	CENZOIC ERA — People evolve

DINO TEETH

a HUMAN TOOTH

DA

MAIASAURA

BIG BOOK OF DINOSAURS

Use your stickers to decorate the landscape.

Phoebe leads us back to Quacker's nest.
He runs to his mother and the rest of his herd.

QUACKER IS BACK WHERE HE BELONGS.

THANK GOODNESS!

Just then, the Magic School Bus comes to pick us up. "Nice work, class," says the Friz.

Use your stickers to decorate the landscape.

Use your stickers to decorate Ms. Frizzle's classroom.